Thanks to
Bishop Ludden for Books
2002-2003

Aunt Claire's
Yellow Beehive Hair

by Deborah Blumenthal
pictures by Mary GrandPré

Dial Books for Young Readers
New York

Published by Dial Books for Young Readers
A division of Penguin Putnam Inc.
345 Hudson Street
New York, New York 10014

Text copyright © 2001 by Deborah Blumenthal
Pictures copyright © 2001 by Mary GrandPré
All rights reserved
Designed by Kimi Weart and Mary GrandPré
The text of this book is set in Cochin
Printed in Hong Kong on acid-free paper
1 3 5 7 9 10 8 6 4 2

Library of Congress Cataloging-in-Publication Data
Blumenthal, Deborah.
Aunt Claire's yellow beehive hair/by Deborah Blumenthal;
pictures by Mary GrandPré.
p.   cm.
Summary: A girl seeking her connection to family past and present
creates a special book in tribute and remembrance, leaving blank
pages for future memories.
ISBN 0-8037-2509-4
[1. Family—Fiction. 2. Memories—Fiction.
3. Scrapbooks—Fiction.] I. GrandPré, Mary, ill. II. Title.
PZ7.B6267 Au 2001
[Fic]—dc21   99-086366

The art was created using pastels.

To Grandma Sophie and Annie,
and my Sophie and Ralph
—D.B.

For Joe, Max, Nicole, Robbie,
and Zach . . . may your family tree
bear the sweetest of fruits
—M.G.

Whenever our whole family
gets together
for someone's birthday,
or a holiday,
or just for the fun of it,
we share a big meal,
then eat and eat desserts.

After we're so stuffed
we can't eat any more,
the grown-ups push back
their chairs from the table
and talk and talk
about the people I see
only in old pictures.

"No! Rose *didn't* have a pug, she had a Pekinese."

"After the big fight with Grandpa, Grandma threw
her wedding ring out of a bus window, but she *didn't* find it."

As all the stories are told,
bits of the past
slip together
like beads strung on a necklace.

I want to know about
the family
who came before me,
the ones I see
only in pieces, in scattered pictures,
family who can't come to my house
or eat with me.
I want to reach into the past
and bring them closer to me.

So one afternoon
when the rain is pouring down,
everyone is home,
and Great-Aunt Ray is over
from across the street,
Grandma Marilyn and I decide
to hunt around
for what she calls
our family "memorabilia."

That means things
to help you remember the past,
like pictures and letters,
postcards and passports,
pressed flowers and old wedding lace.
So we search around
and find things
in shoe boxes,
dusty albums,
old straw baskets,
and the backs of drawers,
and we put them all
side by side
on our big kitchen table.

"Oh, Annie, that was Aunt Claire's purple hair ribbon.
She had yellow beehive hair,
sharp red painted nails,
and a deep, throaty voice."
Then Grandma Marilyn tells about how Aunt Claire
sold face creams and lipsticks
that she cooked up in silver pots
in her kitchen.
She swore that her magic flower creams
would make women so beautiful,
no one would recognize them!

$\mathcal{G}$reat-Aunt Ray finds
Uncle Charlie's war medal and photo.
He had a round, shiny head
and big, thick hands.
Everyone was scared of him
because whenever he came over,
he pinched your cheek so hard,
it turned purple
and you'd have a face-ache all day.

This is Great-Grandma Sophie.
Everybody called her "Sunny"
because of her smile.
I take her lace veil
and put it over my head
the way she wears it in the picture
taken the day she got married.
She grew up on a farm in Sweden.

Whenever Sophie's family needed milk,
she took a bucket from the kitchen,
pulled on a sweater,
walked across a snowy field to the red barn,
and got milk from the black-and-white cows,
all by herself.

The picture in the silver frame
is from Great-Grandpa Louis to his wife.
Great-Grandpa Louis had thick black hair.
Everyone called him "the handsome one."
He used to go to the race track and bet money
on which horse would be fastest.

Great-Grandma Sadie stayed home
and sewed tiny silver sequins onto dresses
and baked twisted breads
to make back the money
that Great-Grandpa Louis lost
when he guessed wrong about the fastest horses.

$\mathcal{G}$randma Marilyn's wedding bouquet is here too,
the pale dried flowers all crinkled and crackly.
"It still smells of roses," Grandma Marilyn says,
"if you press your face up close."

Our family is everywhere on this table,
and some of our things
are so old, brown, cracked, and dusty,
and from so far away
that only Great-Aunt Ray
can explain them to us.

Some of the pictures
she can't look at for too long.
They show men whose faces
make her eyes turn sad.
"They left home to fight a war," she says,
"but they never came back
and saw their families again."

Slowly our album comes together.
We use clues
like dates
and backgrounds
and notes in scrolly, faded handwriting
on the borders of dried-out yellow letters—
and after laughing about the mustaches,
the big-brimmed detective hats,
the movie-star overcoats,
the right-at-you stare of round-eyed babies,

and the stamps from places
hard to find on our globe,
we piece together
a family.
Our family.

We work
to fit everything together,
to make an album
that tells our family's story.

Next to everyone's photos,
I write down what everybody says about them.

Shirley worked
ay and night to send
children to school.

Julius went to
jail for stealing
a horse.

Clara played th
like an angel.

Harry's dark eyes
broke women's
hearts.

olin

David crossed the mountains to escape.

Stella's holiday dinners kept the family together.

By the time the
chicken is on the table,
we have a book
with everything
where it belongs
and everyone together.

Grandma Marilyn says
our book is like the Kaddish,
a prayer of love
to keep the past alive
so that it will never be forgotten.

Everything is included—
pictures, stories, treasures,
and the memories
that go with them.

But our book does not end.
It has blank pages—
white sheets to hold the future,
with room for us to grow.